MONSTER baby

Lee Carr and Jane Massey

RED FOX

Jake was waiting. It was nap time for his little sister, Meg, and it was his turn to play with Mum.

"I'm ready," said Jake, but the phone rang.

Ding-a-riiiiiiing.

"I'll get that and we'll play when Meg falls asleep," Mum said. "If she doesn't take a nap, your sister turns into a real monster!"

"A monster?" thought Jake.
He checked on Meg. She wasn't sleeping.

Jake whispered, "Go to sleep!"
and counted to ten.
But when he peeked into the crib . . .

eeeee!"

Meg squealed and grabbed at Jake's hair.
She was becoming a **real monster!**

"Crazy Monster Baby!"
Jake said. "Go to sleep."
She pointed at
Bo-Bear-the-Dragon.

Jake tucked Bo-Bear into the crib, but **Monster Baby** . . .

"Crazy **Monster Baby**!" Jake said.
"Just go to sleep!"

"**Rub-rub! Rub-rub!**"
grunted **Monster Baby**.

Jake sighed. He really wanted to
play with Mum – but how could he
with a **monster** in the house?

Jake gently rubbed
Monster Baby's back. She lay down.

And just when Jake thought
Monster Baby was finally sleeping,

her ears started smoking,
   and she started **growing** . . .

and **gr**o**win**g until the crib began to

cree**ea**a**aakk**!

Jake heard Mum
coming up the stairs!
He started singing
to cover the noise . . .

And Mum walked by.
Jake had to get
Monster Baby
to sleep before
Mum saw her!

He sang louder
and louder . . . .

And as Jake sang,
Monster Baby
started to shrink.

Her ears stopped
smoking and her fur
disappeared.

Her claws and fangs
vanished

and an adorable baby girl
lay napping.

Jake didn't have to wait any more. He kissed Meg
and ran downstairs.
"Ready to play?" Mum asked.
"Is your sister sleeping?"

"Like a baby." Jake smiled.

"Like a baby."